TABLE O

'The Deep State: The Novel'
- JEREMY STONE

Introduction

"The very word "secrecy" is repugnant in a free and open society; and we are as a people inherently and historically opposed to secret societies, to secret oaths and secret proceedings. We decided long ago that the dangers of excessive and unwarranted concealment of pertinent facts far outweighed the dangers which are cited to justify it. Even today, there is little value in opposing the threat of a closed society by imitating its arbitrary restrictions. Even today, there is little value in insuring the survival of our nation if our traditions do not survive with it. And there is very grave danger

*that an announced need for increased
security will be seized upon those
anxious to expand its meaning to the
very limits of official censorship and
concealment. That I do not intend to
permit to the extent that it is in my
control. And no official of my
Administration, whether his rank is high
or low, civilian or military, should
interpret my words here tonight as an
excuse to censor the news, to stifle
dissent, to cover up our mistakes or to
withhold from the press and the public
the facts they deserve to know. For we
are opposed around the world by a
monolithic and ruthless conspiracy that
relies on covert means for expanding its
sphere of influence--on infiltration*

instead of invasion, on subversion instead of elections, on intimidation instead of free choice, on guerrillas by night instead of armies by day. It is a system which has conscripted vast human and material resources into the building of a tightly knit, highly efficient machine that combines military, diplomatic, intelligence, economic, scientific and political operations.

Its preparations are concealed, not published. Its mistakes are buried not headlined. Its dissenters are silenced, not praised. No expenditure is questioned, no rumor is printed, no secret is revealed. No President should fear public scrutiny of his program. For from that scrutiny comes understanding; and from that understanding comes support or opposition. And both are necessary. I am not asking your newspapers to support the Administration, but I am asking your help in the tremendous task of informing and alerting the American people. For I have complete confidence in the response and dedication of our citizens whenever they are fully informed.

I not only could not stifle controversy among your readers-- I welcome it. This Administration intends to be candid about its errors; for as a wise man once said: "An error does not become a mistake until you refuse to correct it." We intend to accept full responsibility for our errors; and we expect you to point them out when we miss them.

Without debate, without criticism, no Administration and no country can succeed-- and no republic can survive. That is why the Athenian lawmaker Solon decreed it a crime for any citizen to shrink from controversy. And that is why our press was protected by the First Amendment-- the only business in America specifically protected by the Constitution-- not primarily to amuse and entertain, not to emphasize the trivial and sentimental, not to simply "give the public what it wants"--but to inform, to arouse, to reflect, to state our dangers and our opportunities, to indicate our crises and our choices, to lead, mold educate and sometimes even anger public opinion.

This means greater coverage and analysis of international news-- for it is no longer far away and foreign but close at hand and local. It means greater attention to improved understanding of the news as well as improved transmission. And it means, finally, that government at all levels, must meet its obligation to provide you with the fullest possible information outside the narrowest limits of national security. And so it is to the printing press--to the recorder of mans deeds, the keeper of his conscience, the courier of his news-- that we look for strength and assistance, confident that with your help (The

Media) man will be what he was born to be: free and independent."

- **John F. Kennedy Waldorf-Astoria Hotel on April 27, 1961. "The President and the Press Speech" When exposing and warning of the perils in our society regarding 'The Deep State'.**

DISCLAIMER:

"This book was written to entertain and illuminate the public on the elusive subject known as 'The Deep State'. Although it is not a Chronology or an historical reference on the Deep State, It is based on very real, but very often hard to accept realities. You may be entertained at first, but once you decide to accept it as reality, you will no longer be 'A

Deep State Victim', which is their Globalized mission, instead you will become Illuminated, no longer being inferior and ignorant, but becoming equal to them." - **Jeremy Stone**

The Wooden Owl

Deep in the dark of night, deep in a wasteland beyond the prying eyes of civilization, hidden deep in the vast recesses of clandestine wildernesses, lies 'The Deep State.'

On July 15th, 2016 I was abruptly awoken by the Society's own hotline ringing and buzzing on the nightstand. I did not answer. I stared at the phone, watching it slowly buzzing off the nightstand. Time slowed down; I knew it had to have been 'The Company's' operations director giving me a high-level directive. I was on call and startled. The phone hit the ground still ringing. I quickly collected my composure, while prepping my best Governmental monotone voice, I answered the call. Before I managed to say hello, a notably encrypted and garbled voice relayed the message, "I need you to drop this call and call back on the encrypted VPN line, ready to take notes and to follow up where we have left off."

I fumbled through my nightstand frantically, found a pen and notepad and began dialing. "I am ready."

"The gathering is approaching. You are to report to Lodge one-thirteen at 11 A.M on Monday the 16th of July, the night of the Harvest Moon, where you will be escorted to the gathering. Be uniformed in the traditional Bohemian attire. Any updates will be texted to you with end-to-end encryption. Texts will dispatch after being viewed. Respond."

"Understood Sir, I will be there," I said in a forced and measured tone.

The line immediately went dead. This was not my first time receiving a call like this. I was a high-level player in the bureau and held in very high regard with 'The Company.' I knew exactly what this was about; I had been briefed about a meeting to be arranged regarding the importance of forming an 'insurance policy,' which was a phrase that had been floating around the bureau for weeks as the 2016 Presidential election was quickly approaching. I was promoted in rank in both the Bureau and the Company decades ago, and I am considered by many to be the best investigator in the world. I have always declared myself as an Independent to the Company but made a formal request to be known to the public as a Republican. I knew that politics could someday play a role in the work I would be doing with 'The Company,' so being known privately as an Independent made sense. However, I am not a Republican or an Independent. I am a nonpolitical agent of 'The Deep State,' and my loyalty was a strict and fervent commitment to our mission to destroy and subvert any person or organization who would have us undermined or destabilized in any way. I knew this could lead nowhere and if we were found out, everything would lead back to me and my longtime friends at 'The Company.' I've always played the game and played it well, maybe a little too well, because I never thought I'd be in the potentially compromised position that I now found myself in.

As the night of the Harvest moon approached, I grabbed my ticket and luggage with the Company's attire ready to change into; I was headed to lodge One-one-three, which everyone in 'The Company' understood to be The White-Water Lodge in Little Rock, Arkansas.

I took an oath not only the Bureau, but I also took an oath to 'The Company.' The Company was a special division of The Bureau now known to everyone as 'The Deep State.' I believed I knew what I was getting into when I made the pledge to honor the sanctity of the 'Secret Society', but I never anticipated, nor did the thought cross my mind that I would ever see the day where an outsider would become nominated as a Presidential candidate, one running for the office of POTUS - whose veins did not run with those of the Holy bloodline, nor in keeping with the Company's Holy Tradition. Although I secretly had no personal ominous for the newly nominated Republican Candidate, I could not under any circumstances let myself be compromised.

I arrived in Little Rock, Arkansas not knowing exactly what to expect. I knew I would be restrained, blindfolded, and drugged to ensure the clandestine location of the lodge. As I began calculating anything I might encounter I...

"Inspector, get your things and come with us."

A hollow voice commanded behind me.

"Yes Sir," I said suspiciously.

"Could I get an I.D. or badge number, this is my first time visiting." I knew I was out of line, but I was suspicious about another possible rouge agency tracking us.

"We are with Company one-one-three, you know the drill. Now get your things."

I was escorted and manhandled into one of our standard government issued, prototypical black SUV's. As I took my seat, I was immediately restrained and told not to panic. I did indeed know the drill. I closed my eyes and clinched my hands. They understood I was bracing myself for what was to come, and told me not to worry, that this was just protocol, that I would be blindfolded and temporarily drugged to protect the top secret location of the lodge.

I woke up in a drug induced stupor, mumbling incoherently. I looked around and became aware that I was now outdoors and adorned in a grey sackcloth cloak and seated in pitch black darkness, yet I had no fear in the company of my Bohemian brothers.

This was no ordinary gathering. This was indeed a remarkable event; it was June 20, 2016, the first full moon solstice in 50 years, the moon was a beautiful blood red which illuminated the night sky. The beautiful and majestic forty-foot owl was made of oak, which was surrounded by a fire pit. The fire was being reflected on the lake around what could have only been the most elite, and the most powerful and influential leaders of the world. Only the highest ranking in 'The Secret Society' could be in attendance on this exceptionally rare occasion. This must be the Bohemian elevation ceremony. Someone's status was going to be elevated today. Someone will be made today, I thought. That man could only be me.

The cold chant began in unison.

"The owl is in his leafy temple. Let all within the Grove be reverent before him."

"Lift up your heads oh ye trees and be lifted up ye everlasting spires. For behold! Here is bohemia shrine and holy are the pillars of this house. Weaving spiders come not ye here!"

"Members of Bohemia arise. Stand at attention and give reverence to the 'Wooden Owl,' who will soon be illuminated by the anointed one."

The anointed one could only mean two possibilities in my mind. One being the high priest without name, or 'Candidate 2' as we formally referred to the next Queen and high priestess who was chosen to govern this already "Great" Nation. She had the bloodline that was required by all members of the Society to become the next President of the United States. Any outsider who did not have the blood of Kings flowing through his veins would be deemed unacceptable for our Secret Society. There were some throughout our nation's history who slipped through the cracks and managed to beat the systematic, timeless and very effective techniques that have been used by the society for two hundred and forty years, at least in this country. Those who bypassed our ways were also methodically given a subsequent insurance policy. However, previous attempts to subvert our sacred traditions and way of life have ultimately failed all those who previously attempted to thwart and undermine our ways. If this were Madame Secretary, it would be the first time any woman would have set foot on our sacred Bohemian grounds without being then offered at the Alter of The Owl to be sacrificed.

I looked just to my right and saw what appeared to be a high priest adorned with white sackcloth, slowly walking towards the lake. He was hooded with a white cloak with a torch ready to ignite the eternal flame. As the light ignited the eternal flame, sparks flew violently, illuminating the Sacred Owl. Fireworks proceeded, Illuminating all in attendance. A boom was heard across lake followed by a loud voice saying, "Give reverence to the anointed high priestess who has served us so greatly for many years." Everyone unveiled their cloaks. It was the same woman 'Candidate 1' so affectionately referred to as 'Crooked H' standing before us, in all her glory.

She began giving reverence to the wise and eternal Holy Owl.

"I honor thee, I worship before thee, and I sacrifice before thee daily. It is an honor to speak before the wisest of all, give me the dark wisdom which has been passed down from generation to generation, through the ancients, and before the council of the Bohemians, I say, today we are shattering that glass ceiling, and replacing it with a new but equally powerful tradition. As a woman I am so very proud to say, I will be your first honorable woman servant, and high priestess. Accept me and give me your blessing and anointing! Honor me as I have you and make me your Queen! I will honor you now with this precious sacrifice. We know you glory in children, so I have thy knife and thy child to offer before thee! I shall raise my hand and slay! Give me your blessing!"

White Water Lodge

When the elevation ceremony ended, we marched single file sixty-six yards into the adjacent White-Water Lodge. It was magnificent and far more elaborate than any Church of Satan that I had ever seen. We've all heard the stories about the new location where only the elite and High-level priests were welcome, but I never imagined a lodge like this! The vaulted ceilings were thirty feet high with pillars at every corner, marble floors, ornate and decorative domes in every room. Everything was gold plated, and the ancient owl was represented gloriously everywhere in petrified redwood oak.

We were motioned downstairs into a lower chamber which I estimated to be about thirteen feet underground. There was a stone round table at the center of the great room, but this was the largest one I've seen by far, it appeared to be fifty feet wide, but I knew of the old masonic metrics. All measurements were based on the holy number 6, not 5. Masonic weight was in pounds but measured by 6.66 % of a standard pound. And thirteen was the 'Masonic Dozen,' not twelve. The Bohemian round table, where I was seated was sixty-six feet around. I have never seen anything like this in my lifetime. This was an unprecedented but glorious scene for anyone, especially anyone of my stature within The Company to behold.

When an investigation is launched under false pretenses, my job is not to investigate, but to smear. I was not in the smearing business. That was typically delegated to a professional smear artist. I only knew of a handful of men who had the talent necessary to work under the Bohemian club's elite. I could only be invited to this gathering for one reason, and that being, to be elevated and promoted to conduct some sort of investigation, I presumed this could only be a political one.

The roundtable room was now illuminated by an orb which was set directly over the serpent circle. All members uncloaked, and I could immediately see everyone assembled were the highest-ranking officials from every nation in the world. World leaders, diplomats, global financiers, political Pitbull's, Team Hill, and 'O' himself were here.

The high priestess entered the room, but not adorned in white as in the gathering; she was now wearing a low-level grey sackcloth cloak. The High priest was there, also known as the holy one without name. "High priestess, face the high council and remain standing giving reverence to the High Court."

Thirteen Judges entered the room, walked up to their elevated bench and took their seats. It seemed to me the layout shifted from a roundtable meeting to an inquisition. The High court was being assembled, and we were now the jury to cast our votes at the roundtable. The satanic circle was drawn around the high priestess. She sighed and grumbled as the high council looked down at her in judgment.

"We are here today to convene and vote on the progress made by you, high priestess. As all members of Bohemia know, she has been anointed Queen, not only being the first woman in our history who has ever stepped foot on these holy grounds but the first high priestess in our history. This itself defies all previous law, setting a new precedent. We have also been informed that internal polling indicates something wildly different than what was expected of you, being the anointed. You are here today, High Priestess to explain yourself. Many of us are losing confidence in your ability to connect with the people, and we have our doubts as to whether you are following protocol according to our ancient traditions and question what your relationship is with the Spirit. We would like to hear your reason for failing us?" The priestess' face turned noticeably red, and she appeared very disturbed by what was alleged.

"Holy Council, I have the utmost respect for the court and reverence for everyone in attendance today. I must however respectfully rebuff thee. I have faithfully worshiped here and adhered to the laws of our secret society. My blood is the blood of Queens and Kings of old, I have spilled blood to be offered on the altar. No one has offered up more to the Great Spirit than I, not even our very own '44' has worked harder, like a demon, to keep my status in good standing before this council. I can tell you that I have very often communed with the spirit for wisdom. I will win because it is mine alone to attain. The office of this Nation awaits me. If I lose it is will not be my loss to bear, but the loss of this Company'. Where is your faith?

"Do not question the faith of this Court, you are out of order, and we will now vote in the presence of the eternal spirit, whether to uphold you as the anointed or to have you replaced for another, more capable candidate.

Distressed, she cried out, "Wait! I beseech thee; I have an 'Insurance policy' to offer to the Court. I beseech thee, high priest, to withhold judgment."

"Present your 'insurance policy' in detail before the court."

"In the event that I lose the election to 'T', I have prepared a team of the finest spies, smear artists, inspectors, and have worked alongside '44' to compile a report, giving us reason, under the law, to ensure that 'T', the lowly man who does not possess the holy bloodline, as I do, will be shortly thereafter removed from office. I beseech thee to review every member of my team and to put into consideration that 'T' is already under surveillance and will soon be under investigation."

The Council then called all members to cast their vote on whether to allow her to remain the Candidate for the highest office in the land.

We cast our votes. I didn't like her. I knew she could bring every one of us under scrutiny or even prison. I was betting on a coin toss, and I didn't like her odds. My loyalty, however, was first and foremost to 'The Company,' and I felt the spirit move me to vote for her to remain anointed. I had a feeling the council shared the same sentiments.

The votes were cast into the skull and tallied by the High court.

"The votes cast by the council has been tallied. The high priestess will keep her Candidacy for office; however, it is the judgment of this high court, that you are now under probation until your worth has been proven. You will maintain your status in line with our eternal sacred laws, but we are prohibiting your presence within this Society. All future gatherings will be held without your presence, and with that, this Inquisition is hereby adjourned.

Mind Control

"Open your eyes, Mr. McKenzie; I want you to tell me how you feel?"

"I feel fine."

"Do you know where you are?"

"I'm here at the rifle association, with some friends."

"That's right Mr. McKenzie, can you tell me how you got here?"

"I drove here, I think – I can't remember."

"Are you having a good time?"

"I'm having an incredible time.

It's good to be with so many conservatives and patriots."

"Mr. McKenzie, I'm going to count backward from Ten... Nine ... Eight... Seven... Six ... five ... four ... three ... two ... one! You are now in a complete state of awareness and fully conscience, now fully aware of your surroundings."

"Where the hell am I, and who the hell are you!?"

My name is William Baker, Mr. McKenzie, and you're strapped to that chair for your own safety. You've been charged with some very serious offenses young man, and I'd like an explanation from you as to your whereabouts. We need some clarification, McKenzie. You were last seen in Montreal, Canada - honeymooning with your wife Katie McKenzie, just before the murders."

"Murders?! What the hell are you talking about, Are you saying I murdered someone?!?"

"We just want to ask you a few questions son, do not panic. Do you remember what you did just after your leaving Montreal, flying into Atlanta?"

"I have no idea what you are talking about William, I have never been to Montreal in my life, and I don't plan to. I'm an American, I wouldn't go to Montreal to visit a bunch of tree-hugging commies if you paid me! You have me confused with someone else, now get me the hell out of this chair and take the tape off my eyelids you psycho, what is this!?!"

"I'm not sure how it is you don't remember being in Montreal, but I think these pictures may help jog your memory."

Mr. Baker presented Mike McKenzie a dozen glossy, high definition pictures of him and his wife in the heart of Montreal. The images showed the two of them smiling, laughing, affectionate, and they were absolutely not fake. They were real, and It was his wife Katie in the pictures. Nothing in the pictures could have been superimposed; even the best photoshop artist couldn't replicate that kind of detail. The resolution was clear and yet he had no recollection of the event whatsoever. The mind control was used with hypnosis and torture, and it was working. The goal was to break him down to nothing, much the way a good drill sergeant does to a recruit in the military. The same idea is used here, 'ego down' as it's called in the military, and it's also used to bring a man's ego down, then quickly building it back up, leaving their personality intact, while turning them into soldiers. With the Intel agency in charge of the MK 2000 program, breaking down a man's ego was being used for a far more sinister purpose. First, the subject was broken down with standard mind control, which is nothing new, its used every day, but when used with hypnosis and psychotropic drugs, a subject can be blackmailed to do things, even horrible things against his will. All of which were acceptable for the greater good of 'The Society.' They were indeed patriots. In the past, we've used all types, some Democrats, some Communists, Socialists, etcetera, but this would be the first true Conservative subject we've had to go to work on. We picked him up just outside of a Rifle association club rally, invited him to a phony 'high ranking members-only dinner party,' drugged him and made him our permanent subject. He didn't have a chance. We had him carry out whatever it was we asked of him, and in a fairly short period of time too. We funded his wedding, his honeymoon, the over-priced wedding ring for his bride to be and made him look important. His wife thought he worked for the government. When McKenzie left the house for work, he then came into our hypnotherapy office bright and early, day after day, week after week, always believing he was working for the Bureau and that he was an important member of society. He didn't know it yet, but he was far more important than anyone of us, all we ever did here was shuffle some files around to look busy, but McKenzie was our secret weapon and prized possession. We hadn't conducted a successful mind control operation since the sixties. Back then hypnotism was 'all the rage,' it was incredibly popular then, today you'd be lucky to find a hypnotherapy office anywhere in America. MK-Ultra was incredibly successful because we had all the very best Hypnotherapists in the world at that time. We didn't have to look further than 10 minutes outside the beltway of

D.C. to find people who could do the job, and do it properly. This time we had to use an elaborate recruitment program, courtesy of Madam Secretary, who had extensive contacts all over Russia, Ukraine, and the Baltic region. She knew all the best hypnotherapists. William Baker was actually a Russian by the name of Gregor Demitrieriv. Baker was a more natural sounding name for the subject to commit to memory and pronounce, and we thought it sounded a little more believable for the subject. Baker was also undergoing regular hypnotherapy treatments himself. Paradoxically, we even had the guy doing the hypnotizing being mind-controlled to forget he had ever hypnotized anyone.

"Mr. McKenzie, I want you to look at this coin, it's a 1951 Silver dollar. The year isn't important Mr. McKenzie, what is important is that whenever you see a Silver dollar like the one I now hold in my right hand, this will be your cue, Mr. McKenzie. Your cue to carry out and obey our orders and to kill, Mr. McKenzie. Wherever you are, whether it be at an event with an undesirable political figure or a stranger on the street. Whatever the directive we give you, when you get the cue, you will carry out the crime as directed. Your mind shall never stray back to thoughts of your time here, not the time you've spent here with me, or in this building, or any association with us. Your mind and memory are under our full control now.

You are our programmed subject now, Mr. McKenzie."

Operation Amnesia

Everything that was done inside of our 'Secret Society', which we referred to as simply 'The Company' and now referenced by the public as 'The Deep State', was real and was so incredibly compartmentalized for the specific purpose of creating the illusion that with so many components inside a criminal enterprise would always seem to be too incredibly complicated to be considered true. One couldn't explain it in a soundbite. Any tangible proof, had it been revealed or divulged, would be written off as an incredulous conspiracy theory. We knew the psychology of the masses. Even if the public became aware of every component, they could not prove it connected to any other criminal component. This was the beauty of compartmentalization inside 'The Deep State.' Compartmentalization was incredibly powerful in maintaining secrecy within The Society, but it was not absolute. Over the years Hypnotherapy coupled with Mind Control and psychotropic drugs, it became more and more necessary to leave nothing to chance. Our mind control agents were the best, and so were the hypnotherapists, however they were still human, and flawed.

So, we had the Hypnotherapists Hypnotized, along with the mind control agents. Those agents were then also hypnotized and mind controlled, sometimes to forget, and sometimes programmed to have a specific and selective memory. Our selective memory, our narrative. Even the most loyal members were still human and flawed. Complete control would involve something far more complex and convoluted. The idea of keeping a secret was inherently flawed; we knew it must eventually be eliminated and replaced with something more efficient, something bulletproof.

With mind control, blackmail, manipulation, and hypnotherapy we only could control a secret, but the secret remained in a subject's mind, lying dormant and ready to be revealed to another skilled hypnotherapist. We needed something bulletproof. No secrets meant eliminating the need for lies. We were all clean. We were all cleansed of our deepest, darkest secrets. No guilt, no shame, nothing. We were all innocent, pure and illuminated. If anyone asked us if we were guilty of something we'd done nothing wrong, even under a lie detector test, we would deny it and beat it. In the presence of any jury, we were always believable, never leaving any of the usual tells that give away someone who was guilty. Doing interviews with the media was easy because even if any guilt or shame did cross our mind, it was immediately replaced by another inaccurate and shameless memory. A program. We were angels living in the light, illuminated with truth, and armed with the knowledge which the rest of the world did not possess; they were in left in darkness and lies. We knew all secrets. Secrets involving good and evil. Secrets meant only for the most elite and powerful among us. All of these secrets gave us power, there were things on the earth, in space, in spirituality, and in our history which only we knew. Our knowledge gave us power, but everyone else's ignorance gave us even more power. The rest of society were just small minded people, but we were truly Gods.

The evil kept inside our criminal secrets would not be revealed to anyone outside of the elites for two reasons. The goal of compartmentalization was to keep us pure and guiltless, while everyone else died from the stress of their guilt and shame, we lived on in glory. The second wave of our mission was to eliminate memories and restructure them as new memories which became a constant elevation in God-like status to all those at the top. Our secrets were far too precious to ever be comprised, especially at the highest levels. So, we went beyond mind control and hypnotherapy and began experiments into brain altering procedures. We now had the technology to do it. The mind control brain surgery we did was not about implanting microchips into a subject's brain. That was unnecessary and dangerous, what we did was so very easy. We simply removed the part of the cranium adjacent to the part of the brain which controlled inhibition, guilt, shame, and memory. We had isolated that realm of the mind into one very specific area. It was no larger than a penny and removed effortlessly with a laser. It was not removed at all it was effectively burned out with laser treatment, much the way one would undergo vision correction surgery. Computer programs did all the heavy lifting after the cranium plate was removed, the surgery was typically completed with no complications, very little risk, and in less than twenty minutes. The plate was then set back into place, making a subject infinitely more programmable. We were becoming Gods now inside 'The Company' for the very first time. No guilt, no shame, no inhibitions, open-minded and ready to be programmed. Barry Sueta would be our first subject and guinea pig for the initial trial experiments.

"You're telling me I have a benign tumor inside my brain?" Barry Asked.

Yes, Mr. President, but the good news is it can easily be removed with very little swelling, and you will come out of the operation with a new and youthful vibrancy, that's the beauty of it! There is an upside to this, once the tumor is removed it will never grow back."

"Show me the slides, I'm sorry, but I have a hard time believing I have a tumor in my brain."

Here you are, Sir. As you can see, the good news is the tumor is incredibly small, and if we remove it today, you won't have to worry about it growing and most likely then becoming untreatable."

"What is this, another secret project? Do you do this to all the Presidents?"

"Only the ones with tumors Sir."

"Am I going to die?"

"No Mr. President, quite the contrary. After your brain surgery is complete, you will feel more alive and better than ever sir."

"Are you illuminating me?"

"Possibly sir, you will feel no pain at all Sir, and I don't just mean less pain during your surgery, I mean you will feel very little pain throughout the course of your life, once the operation is complete sir."

"Really, and there's no possibility of damage, I still have to be able to read from a teleprompter ya know?"

"None whatsoever Mr. President."

"If I agree to do this, no one in the press or my administration can know about it, and I mean no one. No leaks, and I'd better have that crack high you promised when this is done."

Once he was under, Barry Suita's cranium was then removed, the part of the brain which gave him control over his own mind was essentially burned, and the metal cranial plate to seal it back into place wasn't even necessary. The bone fit seamlessly back into place. We had our first scandal free President, at least as far as he was aware. He wouldn't slip up anymore about his past, everything he needed to know, we would program it for him to know. Our first test subject was a success. He was now completely under our control. Operation Amnesia was a success!

"Uhh where the am I? Hello? Hello?!"

"You are OK Mr. President; you are just emerging from your surgery. Just relax, you will feel a little disoriented until the local anesthetic and morphine wears off."

"I feel good…I feel damn good. Is Donnie here? Where is Don?!?!"

"Sir?"

I wanna know everything about him, I know he knows something - I know it - find out what he knows…Find anything and everything you can on him, and I don't care how you do it!"

The Smear Artists

"Do you know what we do here?" Andrew asked.

"You mean here…at the Bureau?" Weiss answered.

"Listen, you should know better than anyone what we mean." Andy accompanied me, we had a great history together, we knew the same people, went to the same social events and parties, we both knew Weiss just needed a little convincing, so I was mostly silent playing the good cop. I arbitrated the conversation carefully. I knew he just needed a little nudge to fall in line.

"You have a job to do, and this is bigger than the DOJ or the Bureau. We understand you've been very successful in the past at what you do best, manufacturing lies."

"Screw yourself. Weiss scoffed. You guys are just a bunch of old Republican stiffs over here aren't you, it's all true what they say about you at the DOJ. I thought maybe things had changed. It's still the same conservatives with the black rimmed glasses, right out of the movies. You guys better have a good reason for dragging me in here."

"You have an incredible record, Mr. Weiss. You've taken down the Gambino crime family, that's extraordinary, wow you were really something, but that was twenty years ago, and the only thing you're known for today is being a lowlife smear artist, the best money can buy."

"I work for the DOJ, doing real work in the real world, you pencil pushing pricks better get your story straight - unless you both want trouble, I suggest you back off."

"We need to ask you a serious question Mr. Weiss, and we expect an honest answer. What is it you want, is it the money, because you seem to do well for yourself, or do you want to be remembered for doing something the world will respect you for? We can give you both. Whatever you are making now, multiply it by ten, and it's yours."

"I make almost a million dollars a year, and that's not including kickbacks, I don't know anyone in the bureau who makes that kind of money. What the hell is this about Andy?"

"Mr. Weiss, we don't work for the Bureau, we can give you anything your heart desires as long as you say the magic word, Yes. Our agency has been here since the inception of this country, long before the Bureau or the DOJ, we want you to be a part of our team." Andrew answered in a passive-aggressive tone.

Mr. Wiess sat motionless, not saying a word, he was thinking. We let him digest what was said before applying further pressure. "You are asking me to quit my job and work for this 'agency' to do what exactly?"

"We know things, Mr. Weiss, just like you and many agencies do, the difference between these agencies and us is that we control things, Mr. Weiss," I said handing him a drink. "Please, relax. We know It's a lot to absorb. It's completely up to you. What we can tell you for sure, is that by this time next year, you won't be working at the DOJ, you'll be back in upstate New York working for your old firm, chasing ambulances."

"What makes you say that?" Weiss asked with a tremor in his voice.

"Surely you are aware of 'Candidate 1' and his rise to power?"

"You mean the prick who is running for President? Is that what this is about? He's not going to be President." Weiss said sipping his glass of scotch nervously.

"We have reason to believe he will not only win but when he does he will have you exposed and thrown in jail."

"You work for him?!"

"We work for a higher purpose, Mr. Weiss. No, we don't work for him. We need you to work for us to compile a report. Since we can't find anything on him, he's as clean as they come, which is extraordinary, we can't even get him for tax evasion for Christ sake."

"You've checked his taxes? You've checked it out?"

"Oh, we've checked him out thoroughly, 'Candidate 1' is the Ralph Nader of Billionaires. We're starting to wonder what planet he's from. If anyone can build a case out of nothing, to obtain a warrant to investigate him, it's you, Mr. Weiss. You could make history."

He looked around the room, wondering if the money, the power & fame were worth a lifelong oath to 'The Company' if he agreed there would be no turning back, no way out. Members are for life, giving their soul up to the wise spirit owl who guides his elect. I felt the spirit come over me. Mr. Weiss was being illuminated!

There was no need for words anymore, Mr. Weiss stood up, we shook hands and sealed the deal. We had the best smear artist money could buy on our team now, and it was written all over his face, he was onboard. He was glowing and filled with the Illuminated spirit. His face changed, his eyes glowed with that glorious eternal dark spirit, it was a beautiful thing to witness. Any trace of guilt was already being removed from his spirit. He wanted the same things we did; he wanted a New World Order. Everything he wanted was in line with the same ancient traditions we keep, and although it wasn't required, because he was just a low-level player, we did a complete ancestral check on him. He also had the bloodline of Bohemia running through his veins. Weiss wanted the same destiny for the 'Company' as we did, to keep the status quo of lies and deception, Globalization, Communism, Socialism, income equality for every unsuspecting American, a New World Order. He was a newly converted Bohemian, I loved watching a man's being illuminated, above anything else in this world, and now, He was one of us.

"Society members, meet our new convert, Andrew Weiss! Ha-ha, he's on board boys!"

The board members stood smiling and cheering giving him a warm welcome.

"Congratulations Mr. Weiss!" The DNC Chairwoman blurted out.

"Thanks, Hun, I didn't expect this. I'm honored." Weiss said awkwardly.

The applause went on for a few minutes then we all took our seats.

I still used an old school pointer given to me by '43' for the projection slides that followed, I never liked the lasers the newbies used, they were bad for the eyes.

"As you know I am the inspector of this unit. You are the newest members this unit. You are the best of the best. You are the elite, sworn to a sacred oath. You have been chosen based on your high functioning and superior skills. Skills that will be used in synergy, always compartmentalized, and outside of this room, we don't know each other. Our mission is to slowly but steadily undermine 'Candidate 1' , codename 'T,' and his credibility, his integrity, to wear him and his team down. Folks, and comrades (laughter was heard around the room with Russians being present) I believe the phrase you good men of Russia use is 'Kompromat,' am I saying that right'?"

"Da, you say it right, but you say it with Yankee accent, American cowboy!"

Laughter ensued.

"Ha-ha, my long-time comrades still have an incredible sense of humor! You guys are doing an incredible job, but I want you all to know that you may not, under any circumstances find yourself in the position of being comprised. If you become aware of the possibility of any compromise around the corner, you are to report to other high ranking members or to me to see that we find a way out. Our goal is simple friends; we are to maintain the New World Order and structure as it now stands, to undermine the next POTUS until he is framed and impeached. Imagine a picture frame, Bohemian member's. One that has many damning photographs with misleading references regarding our target. Once connected… and we will leave that to our smear campaign! 'Bulldog' meet Mr. Weiss!" Everyone stood again and wildly applauded these two great men.

"I expect only the very best from you boys. You will be working in tandem, together to frame and smear him using the Gestapo tactics of old!"

"Members, go to work!"

Deep State Insurance

"Are you with Don?!" Barry Demanded.

"No, Goddamnit, my loyalty is only to you, have you lost your mind?!"

Rod said squirming.

Barry didn't like to get his hands dirty. He always made sure his hands were flawless for the cameras. He used the goons from Hill's previous administration to give him a proper beating. They were loyal, experienced, didn't snitch, and were always ready to do a little dirty work.

"You - Republican worm! How do you worms slip through the cracks!? You worked for '43', and now it looks like you will be working for 'Forty-Fiiiive'!!!'"

"My loyalty is not to party!! It's to the company!! I took a blood oath to The Company thirty years ago you -Tranny loving psycho that hurts!" Rod whimpered.

"I can't be too sure any longer about any out of you. What have you done for me? All of you Republicans just wait around in your offices, what do you even do over there?!?! You don't do shit! Not for me. Not for Michelle. Not for my legacy. Not for the future of The Society. Our Goal is to create a New World Order. Did you not pay attention to '41'? He was a conservative, wasn't he?!?! What did he say, Rod?!?!"

"He said that we were to create a New World Order, Black Lightning. I know my place."

"Black Lightning?! You don't know me... Let him go. I'm glad you said that Rod, I'm glad you said that. I need you to find me some recruits! I need you to get as many new Bohemian society members as you can and plant them into the DOJ and The Bureau. The Insurance policy has to be bulletproof, Rod!" I need as many new recruits as your ass can find, loyal to me and buried inside these agencies! I need a clean takedown!!!"

"Go to hell," Rod mumbled.

"Did you hear what I said, Rod? Are we clear?"

"Crystal, Barry. I'll take care of it."

"Remember this beat down came courtesy of the big guy. The big guy in "The Company' Rod. You got lucky. I got a firsthand beatdown from him and never even got a good look at his face. Do you see this black eye? He told me that was just a warning and I had to tell him the same thing you just told me! I said I'll take care of it. He's mad Rod. Goddamn, he's mad! When Don calls us all puppets, I'm not sure how he knows what he knows?! I worked for elites most of my life, doing exactly what the tell me to do, but I swear to God, to Allah himself, that I have never thought in my wildest dreams that a secret society guided by the power of Satan himself would be controlling all of us, giving us regular beatdowns like the one I got last night! When I was getting the shit kicked out of me, I thought about how I'd kick the shit out of you, Rod. That old bad boy Satan, he can pack a punch, let me tell you. My Ray Bans won't cover this shiner Rod. No! And what they did to me after… you don't want to know about it. I'm going to spare you that punishment, mostly because you're not my type. I knew I could count on you, Rod."

"Yes, Sir."

"You know what Rod. Here, the first couple of years in the White House, all I knew from you guys was that I would be given special treatment. You contacted me! You knew I was politically ambitious, a Marxist, a Muslim. Most of those qualities aren't what you would look for in your President because I sure as hell don't control anything around here! Your recruiters tricked me with that blood oath. You never gave me a contract! I was young and too inexperienced to care, but you know what, you gave me a prayer mat in the bowling room where I could worship Allah. I thank you for that. I do. You gave me, a man born in Africa, not a natural born citizen – you gave me a social security number, a new name - of my choosing and a birth certificate! A nobody like me, but I had something, didn't I? I had charisma. I believed in something, and you saw that in me. How the hell did Don know? You tell me that, Rod. What Is he?! How did he know when no one else even suspected it?! I want you to tell me how? What do you know about him? Because now I'm listening in on his personal conversations daily, trying to figure it all out. Who is he? Is he a friend of yours? Is he from the lower earth? Is he a U.F.O from outer space? Tell me who he is and how he knows so much about me?!"

With that, Hil's Hitman backhanded Rod, knocking his glasses to the ground. His face was cut from the fresh smack.

"Listen to me – You may have power over me now, but you're nothing come January twentieth of next year."

"Rod, that's where you are wrong. You haven't thought this through, have you? On January 20th according to the 'dark lord' himself, I keep my status in the society, effectively controlling everything and everyone inside the Bureau and

DOJ! You haven't been paying attention. I will still micromanage every one of you Republican pricks. You'll get the orders. You won't hear my voice, but you will know it's me, and you will still follow my orders, and execute them as I tell you to, or you will suffer the consequences the same way you are now. Answer me Rod, who is he?!"

"He is...."

"Is what Rob? I don't need these goons to hurt you, I can smack you around myself, and I have all day to do it."

"We don't know!"

"What the hell do you mean you don't know?!"
You guys are supposed to know everything.
How is it you work with The Company, the
Bureau, the DOJ, and Intelligence agencies and
you don't know?

All we can assume is that maybe he's
connected to someone inside in The
Bohemian Society. He's not a member, but he
is a businessman, and the man knows a lot of
people, you know that."

"Is he connected to the Russians?"

Why would he be connected to Russians? We
don't believe he is, and what do Russians have
anything to do with this?"

That's all Hil talks about, ask her. She's bothered by his wives being beautiful Russian women. Hil thinks she's still twenty-one, she never grew up. She's jealous of everything about him. We all know she's crazy, but if she wants to manufacture a story about him – a smear campaign – I'm all for it."

Election Day

The Administration made a public announcement that Karry was to take a sudden and unexpected journey into the depths of Antarctica. The forbidden land that the U.N deemed to be off-limits to any civilian, and that no nation shall claim territory to, yet strangely became the epicenter of importance for all those who hoped to guarantee a victory for Hil. The press was understandably baffled at the strange timing of this trip scheduled for a night just before election day, while votes were being cast. The media had some questions. The press secretary was grilled for answers regarding the timing for such expedition to Antarctica during election day.

"Why now? Is Antarctica on Karry's bucket list of places to visit?" The Press Corps laughed.

The Press Secretary had a lame story ready about the urgency to check water levels at the south pole, and to further research the effects of climate change. It was all a trumped up and contrived story to cover for something far more nefarious. Something of great importance regarding the timing of a trip beyond the great barrier wall, and into the depth of the forbidden world known as Antarctica.

On the 7th of November, at 03 00 hours, Karry departed for the forbidden world. Karry did not have permission to visit, even as an official representative of the government. The Antarctic Treaty was established on December 1st, 1959 and required authorization from the United Nations council to visit, even under the guise of Scientific research. The only people who had access to that region of Antarctica were government employees who were already there addressing 'climate change.' The researchers there were being paid for their ignorance. They had no knowledge of what really went on there. Even elite members had no access, nor did Skull and Bones nor 'The Company.' Incidentally, Karry was a long-time member of Skull and Bones and had never been to the south pole, neither did anyone that we knew of, only Presidents and Kings were deemed as acceptable to visit this highly restricted area, and even if they were invited, it was never on such short notice. Karry was a trespasser. He knew it, the administration knew it, and Hil, most of all knew it better than anyone else. That's why she sent him there.

"Is it always this bumpy going in?" Karry asked the pilot.

"Always! Listen, Karry, I hope you know what you're getting yourself into going down here?" "I'm not sure, but I was given an order, the hell if I'd want to be down here on vacation. I've heard stories, but I really don't know what to expect! Are you sure you're headed due south?!"

"Sir. There is no 'due south!'" He said handing him a map.

"What is this?"

"That's a world map, sir."

"It looks like a U.N. map, where are we going?!"

"Sir, I've been here before, please buckle up and sit tight, we'll be there in no time."

The flight became terribly turbulent the minute Karry took his seat, violently rattling out of control. The pilot appeared unaffected then took his hands from the yoke. The engines shut down, and the lights and electricity proceeded to go out. The turbulence ended suddenly. In fact, there was no turbulence at all. The plane didn't even vibrate. It seemed to be sailing or gliding. The pilot had no control over aircraft any longer; we were being guided in for a landing by some unknown force. This anomaly didn't seem to affect the pilot; he was chewing gum and perusing his world map.

"The guardians are taking us in, aren't they?"

"Don't worry Karry, it should be a smooth landing, we'll be there in no time!"

The plane landed. It was a smooth landing as the pilot said it would be. It was a relatively quiet landing also. Peaceful. Strange but peaceful. I wasn't at peace. I was somewhere between fear and complacency. I was doing my job. I had no choice. I was here, we made it safely, just as Hil directed me. Sometimes I wondered how much power she possessed. Was she human? Was she a fraud? Did she have as much power as she seemed to have, or was that just the image she assumed we would blindly accept? I knew one thing for sure about Hil, I could feel it, and I knew it now, she wouldn't be President. Whatever the polls said, whatever all of us Democrats and Company members would like to be true, did not make it true. I knew by tomorrow unless I could persuade the devil himself to do it, she would she no longer have any power. She would not become the next President of the United States.

We were greeted by two gentlemen. They appeared to be just like us. That is until I walked off the plane, I immediately noticed that they were not exactly one of us. They were twice my height; they were 12 feet tall. I knew what they were, and this time I wasn't afraid. I felt numb. Numb and controlled. I knew everything from here was out of my control. This was not the world I knew; this was their world. Whatever it was, and whoever ruled it, I was just an unwelcomed trespasser at their mercy.

I was led by the guardians down a path which led to what looked like a military base. I could see what looked like a small town in the distance with huts, cabins, at least two airports, and a massive structure which appeared to be approximately the size of the U.N. building. As I walked further along the path I could see that this was no military base, I was looking at a great city with buildings, highways, structures, trains, and appeared to be densely populated. They motioned me into an elevator which had no up arrow. We were going down. I felt mildly nauseous going down what felt like ten painfully long minutes.

"You were not invited here; you are an unwelcomed guest. Mr. Karry, why are you here?"

"Dark spirit. Holy one, I kneel before you. I shall not stand in your presence. I have come here great and powerful spirit on the orders of my Government and thy servant, Madame

Secretary. She wants divine and complicit collusion from the most divine; she has asked me to come here and to plead with you directly to interfere in the 2016 election. Please, dark lord, meddle, I beseech thee in our elections with thy incredible power to make Madame secretary President."

You have not only trespassed onto our land, but you are now attempting to humiliate us by asking us to do something in which we are limited, even we the guardians cannot do this, We can do many powerful things, and you will soon know just how much we do control. If you followed the orders of this woman, you were fooled. You know we are good, decent, and have great power, yet you took advantage of this. Why?"

"Yes, lord that is why I have come.."

"Since you knew this you will be punished for this humiliation and shamming. We do not have the power to help you. You are a trespasser and a blasphemer. By tomorrow you will see that she will lose and if we had the power to help we would have already. You have come here to undermine our incredible power over this world. Therefore I tell you, you will see my wrath in 3 days. You are to leave the great barrier in 3 days, never to return! After being banished, you will know that I am the Lord."

Three days passed, and it wasn't long after setting foot in Christ Church, New Zealand, The earth shock. We were hit directly by a massive 7.8 earthquake. I was thrust violently towards the ground. The structure I was in was torn to pieces; I was hit with shards of glass and blocks of concrete, giving me wounds and bruises all over my body and a very noticeable black eye. The guardians were punishing me as they said they would, I would never pass the great barrier again, and I wanted nothing to do with that witch Madam secretary. I was lucky to be alive.

In the Woods

After the big election day loss, everything seemed to turn on Madame Secretary. The Society, Bohemia, the Guardians, even the Democratic party turned its back on the once anointed queen. She was broke. Well, not literally but she had no income or cash flow from the DNC or any of her regular contributors. It was hard to feel sorry for her. Personally, I didn't care anymore. I had a job to do. The irony is we were given our orders to take down Don while she still had some power in the world, now she had nothing. What were we even doing this for? I asked myself that question every day. But the mission would never be scrapped. Was it only to take down Don, or was there a bigger mission that I was unaware of? I started to wonder if we all weren't being played by a woman that had long since been abandoned by everyone who we worked for and other powers outside of our organizations. We were working for a powerless woman. Whether or not Don had the bloodline was a moot point now. He was already in power. Three years from now we'd get it right. We would undue anything contrary to our mission with minimal loss, and remaining clandestine was something held in the highest regard. More important than any mission, was never to allow ourselves to be found out. I began to understand that this mission might be trumped up just for Hil and no one else.

Madame Secretary was drinking. Whiskey made her feel cheap, and scotch was too effeminate for her taste. She drank Bourbon, and right out of the bottle. It made her feel like a man. Just like all the men she despised and hated for so long. She could be just like a man in the respite of the bottle. Bill had a separate place, where he stayed comfortably away from her. During the campaign, they lived together only to keep an appearance of being a loving couple. Now she found herself alone.

So, she walked. It didn't matter where she couldn't drive alone with her condition causing narcolepsy. She walked into the woods. She was looking for answers only the sacred owl could give her. Although she was banished from meeting with The Company, she would not be stopped from communing with him. She walked late into the night, sometimes stopping to rest at a bench, sometimes she'd go beyond the beaten path to stumble into a patch of leaves, passing out with her bottle in hand. Hours later she awoke with a quick sip of bourbon to revitalize her to continue her pursuit.

"Where are you spirit guide?!?! Where, I beseech thee?!?!"

"I am here."

She looked around towards the sound the voice. There was a hollowed-out tree with an owl. It was the Great Owl.

"Spirit Owl I have found thee!"

"Why doest thou trouble me in my slumber?"

You, it is you Holy Spirit Owl, I have not come
to trouble you, but to ask you for wisdom. I
implore you, give me the knowledge necessary
to get my power back. Why did I lose? I
thought I was appointed? What happened?"

"I cannot help you, for thou wilt not listen."

Oh, Spirit owl, I shall listen. I have always
sought your guidance and harkened unto thee."

"The people did not find thee likable, Hil.
Your voice was shrill, and your hair was nil.
You dressed like a man and did mingle with the
Klan. Your skin has sagged, and your eyes have

bagged. You assumed the people to be stupid, and Don was right indeed, you are Crooked."

"No! This isn't true; this isn't true! Did Thou not see how close I was to winning? I won the popular vote! The women and the left loved me! You are not the true spirit owl!"
The Great owl went back into his deep state of slumber. He had nothing more to say to her. She was old news. Yesterday's leftovers. A desperate sycophant. A forgotten nobody. A washed up and spit out two-bit politician. In short, she was a loser.
"Talk to meee!!! Hil Shrieked.

"..."

"OK. I admit I could've done a few things differently! What is my purpose now?"

"You have but one purpose. Take him down, undermine him, have him impeached, and replaced with one of us."

"This is still about me! I have the blood of Queens and Kings running through my veins. Help me to regain what is rightfully mine; I beseech thee wise spirit."

"You forget the most important rule of our deep deception, nay two rules. You work for us; we do not work for you. We elevated you among us, then failed us. Our goal is to maintain and sustain a New World Order; you were simply to be our mouthpiece. You have either forgotten that or never accepted it."

"What must I do to stop him, dark lord?'

"You've failed at stopping him. You must go now, start building a group of mindless bots. People who will believe whatever you tell them. Women, men, and liberals alike tell them that they are free to do whatever they want, make them confused and without law. Make them feel like victims. Make them feel hopeless. Do what you do best. Make them feel pitiful. Rally them against good, make them love evil. Make them fail. Make them poor. Make them ignorant. Take away their freedoms. Take away their words. Give them your words.

Be their mouthpiece, and you will be our mouthpiece. Above all, impeach 45. Reinsert the holy bloodline back into power."

"And if I can accomplish this, then..."

Then we will reconsider your acquisition back to power."

"Thank you, dark lord, thank you for your wisdom."

Out of the Woods

When She arrived back to her Chappaqua estate after a very long walk in the woods, she couldn't wait to tell Bill all the incredible things that had happened to her, and that she still had a shot at the Presidency. However, Bill had a glass of Bourbon in his hand and was noticeably drunk. He was watching FNN intently and smirked as his wife entered the room.

"You know honey, I've been watching your former opponent on TV here all day, and I have to tell you, he is one hell of a natural born politician, he takes every one of his opponents, finds their weaknesses, exposes it the world. I mean everyone - whether they love him or hate him, they take it all in -honey! He's the master brander, hell darling I know you don't like him and all, but you really didn't have a snowball's chance in hell! The man is a genius! I tell you what, I sure as hell am glad I never had to play politics with that man. I would've had to concede the election! You were great sugar, you really were, but you didn't have a chance! He said laughing.

"Oh, now you're a supporter?! You know what Bill, I picked your ass up off the street as a country bumpkin, a country boy from the hills and the hallas of Arkansas! You were a nobody. Just a dumb hick and a hillbilly, I used you to rise to power!"

"You bet you did, nobody every liked you. You knew all the right people, had a membership in every elite club, rubbed elbows with those Bohemians, you read all of your Marxist, socialist and occultist books while you were practicing law, and what good did it do you? NOTHING! I told you to stay the hell away from all that occultist voodoo garbage, but you never listened! I had the one thing you never could learn honey, I had personality, and it was and still is genuine! The President and I both have that trait and hell honey that's not just something you can learn poking your nose in a book! Now I know you're still upset that you lost the election, but I am telling you, you can never, and I mean ever, be me."

"You were electable, Bill. You didn't have personality or charm; they only liked you because you were one of them, a good ole boy, an old-school Southern Baptist, another evangelical racist! That's why they voted for you!!"

"You keep telling yourself that honey, it ain't going to make it true no matter how many times you say it. You know when I was a young man, I had some decency, I could've married any woman I wanted, but you kept coming back for more, you couldn't get enough of Bill's sweet lovin' could you?! Now I have to sleep with every high-priced call girl in town just to get the hell away from you!"

"Yeah well, I cleaned up your messes for you, didn't I? Jennifer, Monica, all of your cheap little whores, I got rid of them. How many people had to die because you couldn't keep your thing in your pants, slick willie?"

You did that all on your own, I never wanted anything to do with your shenanigans, honey I never wanted to be president, that was your dream. You took a good man and ruined him. I should've left you back in Arkansas while I still had the chance."

"You would've been nothing."

"And I would've loved every minute of it! A working class nothing is better than what you did to a good man like me. You made me sleep with all those women, and then you cleaned up the mess? They were decent women. You used me because you wanted to advance your career. Look at you now; you're the nobody. A lot of good that dream did. The political arena was always your dream; you just took me along for the ride. I would take it all back to do over again if I could, you can have your politics. Wanna know a little secret honey? I voted for him!"

She slapped him, leaving her red handprint over the left side of his already red face.

Bill sat down stone-faced, didn't look at her and didn't say a word. He went back to sipping his Bourbon and watching the news, ignoring her like nothing happened.

Bill knew his place. Because of the drinking he took it a little too far, his wife was at the top of the Bohemian hierarchy, he was at the bottom now, among the already used. She could have him bumped off, and he knew it. It wasn't worth pushing her any more than he had. Bill had to get it off his chest - it had been haunting him for so many years.

"I'm going to be the next President, the spirit owl told me so! He spoke to me in the woods, out there while you were watching your idol on TV! The spirit is going to guide me, Bill. I'm running for President in 2020, and this time I'm going to win!!!"

Assassin on the Radar

On March 5th, 2018 Peter Strike received an unexpected call from Madame Secretary directly. She didn't start the conversation with the usual formalities or small talk; she always got right down to business. Peter was growing weary of her, yet still listened to her emotionally charged tirade. Strike owed a pledge of loyalty to The Company and all of those in the society. He was also a prominent member of the most elite, and often questioned how much power this woman really had. She fashioned herself as a high-ranking member of the 'The Company,' and Peter believed that she was still without question, the highest-ranking member of 'The Deep State,' outranking forty-four by far. She talked to forty-four the same way she spoke to Strike like he was nobody. It was clear to Peter that she was still very much in charge, and a nasty woman indeed.

"You still work for the bureau, don't you?"
"All due respect Madame Secretary, what are you doing calling me on an unsecured line?"
"Don't refer to me like that. I excepted more from you. You're making me look bad, botching this whole investigation with your hot and bothered texts with Lisa, now everyone knows. People are saying that it all connects to me now. I started this, and I'm going to make sure that you finish it!"

"What would you have me do Madame?"

"I'll tell you what you're going to do, you're going to get your lazy butt back to the Bureau, and you're going to do a job for me."

"I'm not sure if you read the papers at all but, I don't have too much influence there anymore – I don't think you understand – I'm under heavy scrutiny at the bureau right now. You're not the one who should be worried; they're about to frame me as their scapegoat."

"Pete, listen to me, and listen carefully. You are going to be fine – no one there is going to touch you - I promise you that, I just need you to do one small favor for me."

"Ok, I'm listening."

"I need you to find a patsy using the open surveillance we now currently have in place, to find an unsuspecting American - one that is already on our radar. I need him to be a Republican, an NRA member, a gun-toting white male, someone who can be smeared as being a little crazy, but still a productive member of society. Most importantly, he must be a 'patriot' who is willing to do anything to defend the republic, God, and Country."

"I can do that. After I find him, then what?"

"Have him recruited by an Agent posing as another NRA member, then fully indoctrinated, give him the Sirhan, Sirhan treatment."

"Mind control?!" Strike laughed.

"I don't know that we do that anymore Madame Secretary, we find willing persons to be used as patsies these days. We take them off our radar and let them and do it all on their own. Times have changed, its simply not done anymore."

"Don't be naïve Pete, its done all the time. All the contacts you need will be emailed to you. You'll be working closely with the Intelligence community and will quickly find out just how real this still is."
What is this all about, you want another school shooting?! What is this obsession you have with gun control? What are you running for President again?"

"Hahaha." She cackled that same awful laugh consistent with her pattern of complete disregard for human life and any semblance of respect for the law. She wasn't human.

How many more of these mass shootings are you planning, don't you think you've made your point?"

"Pete, I don't need a lecture from you about morality. Those deaths were those of fine patriots, who were sacrificed for the greater good. Think about how many more lives will be spared in the future, because of what we've done. The AR and similar weapons of mass destruction are dangerous and must be taken off our streets. The way I see it, I've spared thousands more by spearheading an effective campaign for more gun control legislation that will pass and will save lives!"

"I'll do what you direct me to do, Madame Secretary, but off the record, you are one uniquely sick and twisted individual."

"Make me proud Pete, I'd hate to see you with another black eye at the bureau."

The line went dead. Strike didn't know who or what her target was this time. It may not be a school shooting this time. She would more than likely compartmentalize and delegate that information to a 3rd party, which Strike would never be aware of. She was one of the greats at compartmentalizing her crimes, so that any hint of impropriety, were it to be exposed, would always appear to the American public, as far too confusing, then predictably dismissed as just another conspiracy theory. That was the Crime Family's formula, they had successfully used it for decades. The recipe was simple. Compartmentalize every aspect of the criminal activity, use opposing party members to elude suspicion, accuse the enemy of the very crime you commit, and make it impossible to explain in a soundbite. It never failed.

Draining the Deep State

I remembered being lured into a very important meeting with a 'State official', I wasn't privy to any details, I was simply told that this was urgent, that I get to the meeting - and that it could be a matter of 'national security, I didn't question something so serious and figured It was worth looking into. Being a part of something, where I could help serve my country was always something I would be interested in, also being a part of something like this would look good on my resume, had I ever been considered for the incoming administration. I always played it cool on television, but I liked the President-Elect, and I wanted more than anything in the world to serve the country I loved with him, in his administration.

My name is Jeb Seasons, and I was going to live up to my name and the reputation I had built up for so many years. All those years putting away bad guys as a prosecutor was about to pay off, all I had to do was play my cards right, and with a little luck I'd be working with the man I had great respect for, I'd be working for the President. Suddenly serving God and Country took on a whole new meaning for me.

I knew that I had served my country with dignity throughout my life, I had an impeccable record of service, I was well known as a practicing Christian, a man of faith, I always tried to do the right thing, and I dearly loved my country. Unless The Don had lost his mind and chose a traitor like M. Rodney, I would be the next Attorney General.

"Hello Ambassador, it's a pleasure to meet you, I apologize, but my secretary was in such a hurry she didn't get your name?"

"My name is Oleg Gavotorev I am not Ambassador; I am representative of the Federation of Russia. Please have a seat it is great honor to meet you, Mr. Seasons."

"I was told this was of the utmost importance, one that could be of urgent National Security."

"No, No, please Mr. Seasons this is no matter. No one can predict future but God. No one. Important? Yes. This is a matter of importance because, listen please, I want you to work for me on project to help people of my country. Without America, we have nothing. We can work together and be friends, or we can be worst enemy, but together we can save world!"

"Listen here Oleg, I don't know what this is about, but I came here out of honor and trust, believing this was something important. I don't have time for nonsense. I don't know you from Adam, and you've already betrayed any trust we had, misleading me to meet you here, now if you will please excuse me - I'm late for a meeting."

"Not so fast Mr. Seasons, there's something else."

"It better be good, because I'm a man with connections, I might look small but, don't judge a book by its cover, I am not a man to be trifled with."

"Sit down Mr. Seasons. I have no doubt you are a man with powers, but you are about to hear disturbing news. The opposition party sent me here to blackmail you, now that we have met, it's already too late for you. You will be under much inspection, as will many of other cabinet members in new administration; we have set up meetings with many of them under false pretenses as well."

"What do you want?"

"It not what I want, Mr. Seasons, it is what your opposition party wants. I am very sorry to be the one to do this, but I must do my job. The DNC wants you to make commitment to them, not to come after them, not to investigate them, for the work they are doing to undermine and ultimately take down President."

"How the hell are you going to implicate me for having a meeting with a Russian?!" There are millions of Russians in America, and thousands of Americans have had meetings with Russian officials. That is not a crime, Sir!"

"Mr. Seasons I am only doing job. The Democratic party paid me through a prominent British spy. I do not wish you any malice, Sir – but as we speak, they are making a case against you simply for meeting with me, which they will hold over your head. Now you must believe me; I have no reason to lie to you. The other meetings with your officials have been set up and although no one has committed a crime, the very fact that you met with us, you will be framed as being complicit with a foreign government. All bad, but these people are not going to play fair. Why am I telling you this? Because I don't care to see a good man in trouble. As for me, I will be in Moscow tomorrow morning, never to be accountable for any of this. You have been set up and blackmailed Mr. Seasons. I am very sorry for this."

"The DNC is plotting to impeach the President before he's sworn in, why would they do that?!"

"You ask a very good question. It is true; it is not strictly a political motivation. Have you heard of secret society?"

"What secret society, skull and bones, I don't believe in any of that!"

"It makes no difference what you believe Mr. Seasons, in fact, it is far beyond any secret society, it goes further, into the bowels of hell. You are not illuminated. Not to worry, you will know that this is all true at some point. What is most important for you to understand is that if you turn on us, you will lose your position and placed in jail. I only work for this society; I owe them nothing. Unless you want to join The Society, watch your step from here Mr. Seasons, we will be watching you. Good day and good luck."

I will never forget that day. He was right; I couldn't tell anyone because I would implicate myself in a false allegation. Although these allegations weren't illegal, they would without a doubt, find a way to take me down. I had to recuse myself; I knew some of these people and what they were capable of. Mr. Meadowfort and Flint were set up in a very similar fashion which did not result in any collusion, which was the original case alleged, were found guilty of crimes that had nothing to do with collusion. This was all because the DNC arranged all of these meetings to make a case against The President and his team, but this case was based on deception. They organized the meetings with Russian officials as their justification to investigate them for Collusion. Collusion would never be found of course, and they knew it, but this Society believed that if they arrested enough people irrespective of if they were 'colluding' or not, they would eventually create a case based on an elaborate smear campaign.

Even a bungled case without merit might eventually be presented to a Court in D.C. which Bob had a 90 percent conviction rate. If they framed The President well enough to cast doubt into the minds of a corrupt D.C. Jury, he could very well be impeached without committing any crimes at all. I had to do something about it, but I had no idea how, especially without being suspected of crossing the society. I was threatened, set up and blackmailed, but I'd be damned if I was going to give up. I had to find a way to beat them at their own game. So, I did the only thing I could think of; I played both sides. Hell, I did it for years as a prosecutor, this time I would do it playing two of the most powerful branches of Government in our country. At least that is what I have now come to understand. As I saw it, there were not three branches of Government; there were only two, The American branch of government and The Deep State.

I decided to set up dinners with Rod and others in the DOJ regularly to knock them off guard. I had them drink with me. Fine dining made sense, and although I would never join their society, I would gain their trust in creating our special club.

"Good to see you Seasons. Wow, I read what he said about you today, he thinks you're a disgrace! What do you think about that?" Rod said never making eye contact.

"I think he's out of control, now I'm not going to speak ill of my commander in chief, but I think we need to double up on this investigation. I don't like what I see with all this Russian meddling."

"Seasons, You do have good reason to be upset, but we can't let our emotions cloud our judgment. We have to make this a clean, open and shut case."

"I understand that, and I agree it has to be done carefully, of course, we can't botch the case. We need real facts, but hell I see no reason not to double up on the process, he's pressuring me, and I'd like to get down to the bottom of this Rod!"

I had them eating out of my hand. I've been playing both sides for years. It came naturally to me. I was even beginning to beginning to believe I was their friend. I could fool them all day long, but I had to be very careful not to fool myself, they were becoming more aggressive about recruiting me without saying it directly. They began giving me more opulent gifts, offering me loans for things I didn't need, and telling me I had a fine career ahead of me whatever happened. It was absolutely the right time to get to work. I knew what to do now, and it couldn't wait a minute longer. I began compiling a list of possible Deep State members within the DOJ, and The Bureau. After looking through our database, cross-referencing keywords, places, people and events tied to already known infiltrators embedded in the departments I had a list of hundreds of people I would use to drain the Deep State. I was having them all fired. They were not fired by me, of course, I had lower lever friends do it for me. Hopefully I would pull the rug from under them all without being suspect, and finally putting an end to The Deep States involvement in our government once and for all.

Closing the Case

The case was not just a weak case anymore, it was a compromised and bungled case, producing no evidence whatsoever of any 'collusion'. Nothing. It was becoming laughable now. All that we have managed to do was pick up a few key people inside The Presidents campaign, take a few misdemeanors and finagled the law turning them into felonies, contrive more unprosecutable offences for foreigners who would, of course, never appear in our courts, and we knew it, and interrogate the campaign knowing they would slip up and get them on perjury charges. We've done everything we could, but now we were about to be compromised. The bureau was taken apart and dismantled by The President, which was bad enough. He downsized the Bureau by about twenty percent, weeding out countless 'bad actors,' they were good men too. It was something no one anticipated, because it was unprecedented. The press tried to spin it as an infringement of their rights, unamerican, and obstruction of justice. The truth is, it was completely legal and set us back three decades. This was a major blow to 'The Company.' Our reputation was also in question. Almost seventy-five percent of the American public now viewed our investigation as a charade, that kind of public opinion left us wide open to public scrutiny. We couldn't afford it. Inside the bureau there was dissent among the incoming newbie cadets, forming a small, but ever-growing rouge agency. The division alone within the bureau was split right down the middle. Half of the agents were Conservative leaning, and the other half, Democrats.

I was loyal to the cause and everything that was asked of me by my superiors; now it was time to accept small defeat, while it would set us back, we would lose the battle but win the war with a strong end game. A second shot at planting one of our own inside the political arena was right around the corner for us. The President was up for re-election, and we had measures in place that would ensure a victory.

We used the cloud, not voting machines to alter data in key states. The Presidents paper ballot campaign was already worked around by hiring recruits to alter the votes on paper. They actively tampered with early voting via mail and merely shredded the paper ballots in cities that were not under scrutiny. We also had illegal immigrants paid to vote multiple times across state lines. College students would be bussed in from the major leftist colleges around the country, and they didn't even have to be paid to do it. If there were ever any question of what was on paper, it would be deferred to the votes in the cloud, no one questioned it. The Secretary tried to alter the database in the cloud on Election Day, in Michigan, Wisconsin, and Pennsylvania, but she was late! She was always last minute, sloppy and complacent. I never liked that about her. Because of her arrogance I was now paying the price. Everything was about to come down on me, all because of her lack of preparation for a job she could not finish. I will close this case, but there was one final step that had to be done before to make it a clean one. She was the only evidence left that could compromise us all. The Bureau. The DOJ. The Russian/DNC collusion. The Company. The Society. My sterling reputation. She did it now. Madman secretary was the only evidence left. It's up to me to destroy the evidence. I will do it myself; I didn't need permission from The Company or any other group. They would understand once she'd been dispatched. I dialed Christopher Still.

"What's on your mind inspector?"

"Are you still in the game Steel?"

"If you're asking me if I'm interested in some more action – the answer is yes."

"Is 10 million enough action for you?"

"That sounds reasonable."

"Then I'm going to ask you to get rid her - Madame Secretary."

Steel paused for a minute.

"I would've done that for 1 million, but that doesn't go too far these days. I understand she wants to see us all locked up now. Of course, I'll do it, but I want half up front, inspector."

"Bitcoin?"

"What else?"

"You know this will kill two birds with one stone, don't you?"

"How's that?"

"I'd be using my Russian contacts to do it, and that would complete the collusion narrative, wouldn't it?"

"Steel, they told me you were the best, but they didn't tell me you were a goddamn genius!" The inspector said laughing.

"She's giving her announcement speech in Chappaqua tomorrow; can you make it?

"Are you kidding? I wouldn't miss this for the world.

It was that easy. The case was closed.

The Svengali

Christopher Still was the perfect go-to guy for the creation of the dirty dossier, to be used in our secret courts. He was foreign, a former British spy, he had extensive criminal Russian contacts, which meant he'd never be prosecuted in Great Britain, because it was not their crime to prosecute, and we knew he'd never be extradited to the States. We made it a point to have Madame Secretary delegate responsibility to the DNC, who then delegated responsibility to an 'Independent Law Firm' who then hired Christopher Still, who then delegated responsibility to a proxy Russian smear group, who would never be called to stand trial.

Compartmentalization was a beautiful thing. Incidentally, we used 'Independent law firms' across the country as a proxy to get our agenda accomplished, without having to worry about legal responsibility, after all, they were the best legal firms in the country. We had them Independently working with lobbyists, Senators, Congressmen, Governors, the media, paid protesters, it always worked because it was so simple. No one dared question an' Independent Law Firm.' We used sexy young female communication directors who were oblivious to politics, couched with scrips on every possible objection and question that would be posed to them. They didn't know what the firms did, or the corruption behind it. They thought they were talented, getting paid for their skills, being giving a chance to climb the political ladder, working for the greater good, and their victims couldn't question them. They were young and naïve hacks who were paid as temp agents but never signed on as paid employees. If you wondered what a top-down pyramid looked like, we were the perfect pyramidal hierarchy model. The people working at the bottom knew nothing, because they were told nothing. Those in the middle were promised the world; many times, paid exorbitant amounts of money, once their purpose was served, they were spit out with no story to tell. The elites at the top always needed to be fully indoctrinated, most of the time they were already directly related those in power that were already loyal and fully indoctrinated. The higher it went, the more important Hypnotherapy, psychotropic drugs, and complete control became necessary to ensure our secrets were kept secret.

Once Christopher Still got the call from the Inspector to dispatch The Queen of the Bohemian world, he quickly got to work. He dialed Moscow and had the greatest Svengali in mother Russia working for him. His name was Grigori Risputin the third.

Grigori was very well known in Russia, but no one knew him in America. He was a wild card for us because we never dabbled in occultism when it came to mind control. We strictly adhered to what we knew, mind control mechanisms that were scientifically proven to work. Our methods were tried, tested and true.

What Grigori did was like nothing we'd ever done in the intelligence community. The Russians were mystics, psychics, and spiritualists. They used mind control tactics that went far beyond the science of human psychology, going into a mystical realm of Svengali powers. It was too risky for us to rely on these kind of untested and strange tactics, but Christopher Still was working on very short notice and didn't have time to worry about the protocol, especially when it came to murder. Grigori had a penchant for women subjects. He felt they were weaker and easier to manipulate. He used one of his own subjects, a 25-year-old Ukrainian woman named Tanya Verskaya.

"Look into my eyes, Tanya. Stare deeply into my eyes. Stare into my soul. Listen to what my spirit commands you to do and obey it!"

"I am under your spell, always Grigori, you know this. You are my lord and master, I always do the will of my master, lord."

"Look deeper into my eyes, Tanya, what do my eyes command you to do?"

You are giving me an order master, I see it. I see what you see my lord!"

"What do you see Tanya, continue to look into the mesmeric gaze of my eyes, and know my commands!"

"I see a woman, the woman who is running for President. The Witch. I see her. I see her!"

Where is she Tanya, where is she?!

"She is at convention, being held tomorrow in New York. I will go there; I must leave here tonight. I will leave on a great journey to America. I will go to New York, and I will find her."

Christopher Still phoned the Russian contacts who employed the great Svengali, Grigori Risputin.

"Yes, yes Mr. Still we have met with Grigori and told him the orders you have given him. He has taken his subject, one Tanya, who has been under his spell, she was mesmerized by the great Svengali. She always carries out her directives, and she knows what to do Mr. Still. You can relay this message to your inspector; he has no reason to worry. She will carry out the directive. She always does."

"I'm very pleased to hear that Sir, It's difficult getting someone in his league to work for us on such short notice, we are very grateful, and your team will be paid substantially for all of the good work you do for us."

The Game Has Changed

I got a call from Hil early in the morning on November 4th, 2018 she told me she wanted to discuss business and her announcement to run in 2020. She was going to use getting guns off the streets as her campaign platform. I begrudgingly agreed to meet with her. She sounded very eager to talk about something in confidence, and I assumed she used an overly cordial disposition as a smokescreen to keep her off the radar when speaking to me over a non-secure line. This was unexpected, and ironically, I was already headed to see her with some friends unannounced.

This would make things easier for me. I wouldn't have to worry about covering my tracks. She was coming to me. I would do it here, it would be clean, and I'd have 'The Company' make it look like a suicide.

I took a pistol out of my collection, the same model I knew she used, it had the same registration number, the same year, make, and model. The Company members inside the Bureau would take the gun out of her house once the investigation began. I had no choice. She was jeopardizing everyone involved, and now that the case was botched, she had to be disposed of. She was the only witness left against us in the U.S. who could rat us out. She called the society to conduct this mission. She failed, and it was time to clean up the residue. I was now given the OK by the members of Bohemia and was backed by a nearly unlimited group of members, and we were heavily funded.

At 11 A.M. sharp, she rang the doorbell and smiling ear to ear, told me how good it was to see me again.

"Well its been a long time.... years.' She cackled.

"It sure has been, Madam Secretary. Please make yourself at home."

She didn't waste any time.

"I am so proud of you and everything you've done. I know we're going to get that bastard sooner or later, but I came here to tell you it makes no difference anymore whether you are the one to take him down or not, because I'm announcing my run for President tomorrow! I really think I have a chance this time, with the resistance built up the way it has, I tell ya, this time I'm going to beat him. Would you like to know how?"

She was sloshed, already boozed up on my 1000-dollar bottle of scotch. She wouldn't stop. I just listened intently, pretending to be interested.

My commitment to gun control is going to be priority number one. The American people want it more now than ever. Seventy-five percent of Americans want these guns off our streets!"

She was getting close to my gun rack Goddamnit.

"These! These AR-15s" She took one out of the rack and displayed it, as if she were already campaigning. She was a mess. I knew she didn't know how to handle a gun; she had no knowledge of how to operate handguns, much less an AR-15.

"Do you know how dangerous these guns are in the hands of a criminal? Thousands of untold deaths a year are committed by these weapons of war. I fully understand why you have them, of course, you're a fine upstanding blue-blooded American patriot, with the best credentials, a sterling reputation, but in the hands of the average uneducated, gun-toting, conservative, white male hillbilly, these things are dangerous, and very often lethal. Hell, I shouldn't be holding this thing."

Hil took the safety latch off, cocked the gun quickly - it was loaded. She aimed it at me and mowed me down. Thirty rounds to the chest!

"I told you these things were dangerous" She cackled as she dropped the AR next to my lifeless body.

She didn't bother wiping the AR clean. Her dirty little fingerprints were left all over the 'Weapon of Mass Destruction' as she called it, when mocking me. She was sloppy and careless, but it didn't seem to faze her. She knew her elite goons would take it from here. McKenzie, the MK 2000 mind-controlled subject, arrived with his bag of ammunition and his AR arrived within seconds, just as she waltzed out. As he stood over me, his face turned white. He didn't move, he was in shock, still noticeably entranced. The blank and vacuous stare he kept, was surely the work of the intelligence mind program, the professional mind control agents that made Sirhan, Sirhan forget where he was, why he was there, how he got there, and his motive, trained this poor soul to do something he was against and never given the chance to fully execute. He continued staring, as the Agency showed up to arrest him and clean up any evidence that would implicate the Secretary. It was an exceptionally clean operation. Madam Secretary had more than dumb luck; she had some supernatural help. No one was that lucky. 'The Company' was wise to things forbidden to the rest of the peons of the world, understanding things that would drive most ordinary citizens to madness. We kept those secrets with us, we believed ourselves to be an extension of the guardians, though we knew very little of sorcery. She was connected to something far greater. As I lie there nearly gone now, I prayed to a different God, that someone would overtake her in the world of politics, someone that would trump her evil with good.

Hil arrived at her dinner party right on time. She was all smiles being reunited and greeted by her fair-weather friends again. She walked through the crowd feeding off the energy of her adoring fans, none of them knowing what atrocities she'd just committed. She was a faithful and maniacal politician. Those that wanted to see her as a champion of women's rights did. They saw what she wanted them to see, and she was spectacular, reveling in all her devious glory.

"Thank you! Thank you, everyone…who could make it. You know, somehow, I made it. Somehow by the grace of God, after a lot of soul-searching, I found my way out of the woods, and here back with you stronger and better than ever, stronger together! We resisted, persisted, and you enlisted! I want to start by thanking all of you. You stood by me when the world went crazy, when you didn't have a voice, ashamed, I was right there with you, I never gave up, and never backed down. We're all dreamers. We all have something we need to overcome, and this country because of one sick man who let us descend into a kind of red square type of darkness, letting us fight, cause division and strife in this great country – I got news for you, it was already great! Now we have mass shooting – it seems like every time I watch the news there's another one! Gun violence is happing far too often in this country and instead of talking about it – I'm going to get every one of these goddamn AR's, these weapons of mass destruction off the street! Off the street and out of the hands of dangers people! Someone just informed me, that on my way over here, that there was yet another act of senseless gun violence just blocks from here! Another so-called "Law-abiding citizen mowed down one of our men in blue. That sick killer wasn't a law-abiding NRA member at all, as republicans would have you believe; he was a dangerous criminal! Folks I'm going the make sure that no one in America has to live in fear of a dictator in the White House, or a gun-toting NRA member who wants to lie to you about how important it is to have them! I promise you that. Today I'm making that commitment to you. I am running for President because times are tough, they were tough for me too, and like me, you're going to rise from the ashes, out of the woods, and together once and for all, we're going to shatter that glass ceiling!"

A loud boom was heard throughout the convention hall as blue shards of broken glass rained down from the roof of the conventions dome ceiling. Everyone in attendance quickly hit the ground, shielding themselves, not knowing what had just happened. Shots were fired. The shooter was visible to everyone, as she was the only person in the crowd still standing. Something just went horribly wrong, the Svengali mind control operation that had been so hastily and shoddily put together by Chris Still could not be stopped. It was Tanya Verskaya. She was not programmed, she was possessed. She stood motionless and mesmerized, still under the spell of the great Svengali.

The Deep State had been compromised and decimated now, and this time by their own overreaching and greedy hand. It was over for us, at least for now. We had to retreat into the shadows to hide again, away from daylight which now shone brighter than ever before inside our great Republic, The United States of America.

We had become so powerful over the last 250 years, since the inception of our great nation, when 'The Illuminati' was formed, or The Order of Illuminati as it was coined and created by the former Jesuit priest by the name of Adam Weishaupt. Adam was fascinated by the Free Masons and what dark secrets they may hold. He however badly miscalculated who the Free Masons were, and in doing so infiltrated our very system of Governing from our inception, creating The Shadow Government and 'The Deep State.' Weishapts false interpretation of Free Masonry and who they were, gave us the beginning of what we now know as 'The Deep State.' He was the first to embed himself and his indoctrination into our very way of life, under the assumed belief that he was the mastermind who finally cracked the mystery behind Free Masonry – Weishaupt was able to mislead enough elites, just after the Revolutionary War .Yet long before the 'Revolutionary War,' Europeans wanted nothing more to do with any Global World Order. We weren't about to be represented by a bunch of corrupt elites on the other side of the Atlantic, who had no idea who we were as Americans. They knew nothing of the resolve and fortitude of the American people or our unwavering and resolute commitment to freedom. What we possessed was a foreign concept to the Royal Monarchy. We were the freedom fighters, the rebels, the street fighters, the deplorables, and the free thinkers of the world. Our minds were free to choose anything we sought to achieve or realize. We would not be enslaved any longer to an imperialistic government which did not represent us or our plight as a free society. We would set up a representative government, not a Monarchy. The street fighters who would never give up, nor surrender. We wanted nothing more to do with the Church of England, nor would we continue to accept the ways of the Free Masons, who were also by that time, tied to the disconnected elites of England. Although the Free Masons were always understandably misunderstood as being sinister or evil, they were not. Nothing could be further from the truth. The power that the Free Masons held for hundreds of years was simply a direct result of their inherent secrecy. There is great power in secrecy. What do these people know that we don't? Who are they? How powerful are they? Did they control things we could not? The Free Masons did not want to live in secrecy but forced to, out of necessity. Their secrecy was the key to their very survival. As the Masons witnessed 'The Church' becoming unspeakably corrupt, immoral and not at all representative of the people or its Christian beliefs, something went horribly wrong. Something went very wrong for The Church during the middle ages, which was the beginning of the great awakening. It was not free or open to new possibilities, but instead, it became completely controlled and usurped by the Government and then weaponized against its own people. As

The Free Masons came to realize they could not hope to fight such an incredible power with an army or militia, they found a way out, and it didn't involve violence, war, or a revolution. The Masons very shrewdly used the same techniques which gave the now corrupted Church all of its high power, the illusion of having a secret. The Masons built houses, buildings, lodges, and Temples–giving them places to assemble (freedom of assembly). The Church of the middle ages did not allow its citizens to question anything; they didn't even afford them the knowledge of something as simple as how to build something. The Masons had to separate themselves from The Church, going underground, and as a result, they gave us the pillars of our American foundation and freedoms. They gave us freedom of Speech, Freedom of Assembly, The Right to Bear Arms, and the freedom of having a Separation of Church and State. In fact, they gave America all of its privileges. Everything you know in the Declaration of Independence and the Bill of Rights was a direct result of the Free Masons revolt against a Government gone wild and completely out of control - elitism at its worst. Most of us cannot imagine a world where free thought could be suppressed and anarchy and disorder were accepted as the status quo.

The Deep State embedded themselves into our American system in 1776. They fooled many of our founding fathers, because we had very little time to find an alternative to the British Free Mason system of 'Separation of Church and

State.' It was the Free Masons who gave us this revolutionary idea three hundred years before our 'Bill Of Rights' and 'The Declaration of Independence.' The idea of a Governments separation of Church and State was a revolutionary one, yet it was conceptualized in the dark ages. At that time people had absolutely no rights and were completely subjugated by a highly corrupted system which we referred to at the time as simply 'The Church'. It was far worse than any Monarchy or any corrupt Dictatorship, Regime or Communist Governmental system. The Free Masons weren't rejecting God or any religion, but they knew a Government which held all of its power inside one Government sponsored and representative Church - indoctrinating its people, controlling the minds of children to submit completely to them, while killing its citizens, conducting experiments on them, and killing free speech, had to come to an end. The Masons started this rebellion against freedom in the Middle Ages; the founding fathers were just finishing what they started.

The Deep State, on the other hand, is the Illuminati. The theory behind the Illuminati is that spirituality, Gods Law and the law of mankind does not have to be separate. Instead, we could fuse the best of both worlds. We use the deepest knowledge of good and the evil to become Gods. The New World Order is the idea that, in fusing all knowledge, both good and evil, we are able to deceive society at large to believe our version of the truth as accepted truth. Our goal is not a political one; it is very simply to recruit every person on the earth as a member, no matter what their personal beliefs or political associations are - to eventually reach full control with every man, woman, and child as an active participant. The majority of these people never knowing they too are members and willing participants of our 'Secret Society', our 'Deep State'. Science was a lie but loosely fit Gods model of the earth, moon, sun, stars, and creation. We had a new design in place and used it. A new model of creation that would very easily deceive those who would never dare to question it. Isaac Newton was used to spearhead our version of reality, using math and the power of observation, and most importantly 'theory' to explain Gods nature, without God being a part of the equation. We started with Gods laws then worked backwards; Essentially reverse-engineering God. The fact that we as the illuminated elites of society have managed to keep these secrets from everyone else, made us Gods over the rest of the ignorant and poor unsuspecting people of the world. Alchemy was a sham. The search for the fountain of youth and making gold with chemistry of course was a fantasy, but the reassurance that these types of fantasies were even possible gave our small minded subjects hope. Even if it was false hope, we felt it was an essential and necessary lie. We would no longer depend on a God to solve any of our problems or any of the worlds ills, we would use scientifically proven systems that would do that for us. And if fomenting war between nations, even World Wars meant we could attain a New World Order, we would ensure it would become a reality.

The Deep State became so accustomed to never being exposed that they had become arrogant and sloppy when it came to overextending their power, and in doing so revealed it's shadowy and sinister nature to the world. The Deep State was forced to retreat for a time, and by an outsider no less. They retreated back into the shadows, back into the veil of darkness and back into the clandestine wildernesses they knew so well, knowing they were defeated for now, though they would be back again. They always came back for more.

Made in the USA
San Bernardino, CA
19 July 2018